Lincolnshire
COUNTY COUNCIL

discover libraries

Meeting Cézanne

For Pam and Tim, with thanks for wonderful days
at Les Guis, where this was written
M.M.

For Jacques and Odette
F.P.

First published 2006 in *Singing for Mrs Pettigrew: A Story-maker's Journey*
by Walker Books Ltd, 87 Vauxhall Walk, London SE11 5HJ

This edition published 2014

2 4 6 8 10 9 7 5 3 1

Text © 2006 Michael Morpurgo
Illustrations © 2013 François Place

This book has been typeset in Adobe Caslon

Printed in China

British Library Cataloguing in Publication Data:
a catalogue record for this book is available from the British Library

ISBN 978-1-4063-5113-2

www.walker.co.uk

Meeting Cézanne

Michael Morpurgo

illustrated by François Place

WALKER
BOOKS

Other books you will enjoy:

Homecoming

I Believe in Unicorns

Singing for Mrs Pettigrew: A Story-maker's Journey

The Kites Are Flying!

The Mozart Question

This Morning I Met a Whale

I don't remember why my mother had to go into hospital. I'm not sure she ever told me. She did explain that after the operation she would be needing a month of complete rest. This was why she had had to arrange for me to go and stay with Aunt Mathilde, my mother's older sister, in her house down in the south, in Provence.

I'd never been to Provence, but I had met my Aunt Mathilde a few times when she'd come to see us in our little apartment in Paris. I remembered her being big and bustling, filling the place with her bulk and forever hugging and kissing me, which I never much cared for. She'd pinch my cheek and tell me I was a "beautiful little man". But she'd always bring us lots of crystallized fruits, so I could forgive her everything else.

I was ten years old and had never been parted from my mother. I'd only been out of Paris once for a holiday by the sea in Brittany. I told her

I didn't want to be sent away. I told her time and again, but it was no use.

"You'll be fine, Yannick," she insisted. "You like Aunt Mathilde, don't you? And Uncle Bruno is very funny. He has a moustache that prickles like a hedgehog. And you've never even met your

cousin Amandine. You'll have a lovely time. Spring in Provence. It'll be a paradise for you, I promise. Crystallized fruit every day!"

She did all she could to convince me. More than once she read me Jean Giono's story "The Man Who Planted Trees", the story of an old shepherd set in the high hills of Provence. She showed me a book of paintings by Paul Cézanne, paintings, she told me, of the countryside outside Aix-en-Provence, very close to Aunt Mathilde's home. "Isn't it beautiful, Yannick?" she breathed as she turned the pages. "Cézanne loved it there, and he's the greatest painter in the world. Remember that."

A city boy all my life, the paintings really did look like the paradise my mother had promised me. So by the time she put me on the train at the Gare de Lyon I was really looking forward to it. Blowing kisses to her for the last time out of the train window, I think the only reason I didn't cry was because I was quite sure by now that I was indeed going to the most wonderful place in the world, the place where Cézanne, the greatest painter in the world, painted his pictures, where Jean Giono's old shepherd walked the high wild hills planting his acorns to make a forest.

Aunt Mathilde met me off the train and enveloped me in a great bear hug and pinched my cheek. It wasn't a good start. She introduced me to my cousin Amandine, who barely acknowledged my existence, but who was very beautiful. On the way to the car, following behind Aunt Mathilde, Amandine told me at once that she was fourteen and much older than I was and that I had to do what she said. I loved her at once. She wore a blue and white gingham dress, and she had a ponytail of blonde hair that shone in the sunshine. She had the greenest eyes I'd ever seen. She didn't smile at me, though. I so hoped that one day she would.

We drove out of town to Vauvenargues, Aunt Mathilde talking all the way. I was in the back seat of the Deux Chevaux and couldn't hear everything, but I did pick up enough to understand that Uncle Bruno ran the village inn. He did the cooking and everyone helped. "And you'll have to help too," Amandine added without even turning to look at me. Everywhere about me were the gentle hills and folding valleys, the little houses and dark pointing trees I'd seen in Cézanne's paintings. Uncle Bruno greeted me wrapped in his white apron. Mother was right. He did have a huge hedgehog of a moustache that prickled when he kissed me. I liked him at once.

I had my own little room above the restaurant, looking out over a small back garden. An almond tree grew there, the pink blossoms brushing against my window pane. Beyond the tree were the hills, Cézanne's hills. And after supper they gave me a crystallized fruit, apricot, my favourite. All that and Amandine too. I could not have been happier.

It became clear to me very quickly that whilst I was made to feel very welcome and part of the family – Aunt Mathilde was always showing me off proudly to her customers as her nephew, her "beautiful little man from Paris" – I was indeed expected to do what everyone else did, to do my share of the work in the inn. Uncle Bruno was almost always busy in his kitchen. He clanked his pots and sang his songs, and would waggle his moustache at me whenever I went in, which always made me giggle. He was happiest in his kitchen, I could tell that. Aunt Mathilde bustled and hustled; she liked things to be just so. She greeted every customer like a long-lost friend. She was the heart and soul of the place. As for Amandine, she took me in hand at once, and explained that I'd be working with her, that she'd been asked to look after me. She did not mince her words. I could not expect to spend my summer with them, she said, and not earn my keep.

She put me to work at once in the restaurant, laying tables, clearing tables, cutting bread, filling up breadbaskets, filling carafes of water, making sure there was enough wood on the fire in the evenings, and washing up, of course.

After just one day I was exhausted. Amandine told me I had to learn to work harder and faster, but she did kiss me goodnight before I went upstairs, which was why I did not wash my face for days afterwards.

At least I had the mornings to myself. I made the best of the time I had, exploring the hills, stomping through the woods, climbing trees. Amandine never came with me. She had lots of

friends in the village, bigger boys who stood about with their thumbs hooked into the pockets of their blue jeans, and roared around on motor scooters with Amandine clinging on behind, her hair flying. These were the boys she smiled at, the boys she laughed with. I was more sad than jealous, I think; I simply loved her more than ever.

There was a routine to the restaurant work. As soon as customers had left, Amandine would take away the wine glasses and the bottles and the carafes. The coffee cups and the cutlery were my job. She would deal with the ashtrays, whilst I scrunched up the paper tablecloths and threw them on the fire. Then we'd lay the table again as quickly as possible for the next guests. I worked hard because I wanted to please Amandine, and to make her smile at me. She never did.

She laughed at me, though. She was in the village street one morning, her motor-scooter friends gathered adoringly all around her,

when she turned and saw me. They all did. Then she was laughing and they were too. I walked away knowing I should be hating her, but I couldn't. I longed all the more for her smile. I longed for her just to notice me. With every day she didn't I became more and more miserable, sometimes so wretched I would cry myself to sleep at nights. I lived for my mother's letters and for my mornings walking the hills that Cézanne had painted, gathering acorns from the trees Jean Giono's old shepherd had planted. Here, away from Amandine's indifference, I could be happy for a while and dream my dreams.

I thought that one day I might like to live in these hills myself, and be a painter like Cézanne, the greatest painter in the world, or maybe a wonderful writer like Jean Giono.

I think Uncle Bruno sensed my unhappiness, because he began to take me more and more under his wing. He'd often invite me into his kitchen and let me help him cook his soupe au pistou or his poulet romarin with pommes dauphinoises and wild leeks. He taught me to make chocolate mousse and crème brûlée, and before I left he'd always waggle his moustache for me and give me a crystallized apricot.

But I dreaded the restaurant now, dreaded having to face Amandine again and endure the silence between us. I dreaded it, but would not have missed it for the world. I loved her that much.

Then one day a few weeks later I had a letter from my mother saying she was much better now, that Aunt Mathilde would put me on the train home in a few days' time. I was torn. Of course I yearned to be home again, to see my mother, but at the same time I did not want to leave Amandine.

That evening Amandine told me I had to do everything just right because their best customer was coming to dine with some friends. He lived in the chateau in the village, she said, and was very famous; but when I asked what he was famous for, she didn't seem interested in telling me.

"Questions, always questions," she tutted. "Go and fetch in the logs."

Whoever he was, he looked ordinary enough to me, just an old man with not much hair. But he ate one of the crème brûlées I'd made and I felt very pleased a famous man had eaten one of my crème brûlées. As soon as he and his friends had gone we began to clear the table. I pulled the paper tablecloth off as usual, and as usual scrunched it up and threw it on the fire. Suddenly Amandine was rushing past me. For some reason I could not understand at all she grabbed the tongs and tried to pull the remnants of the burning paper tablecloth out of the flames, but it was already too late. Then she turned on me.

"You fool!" she shouted. "You little fool."

"What?" I said.

"That man who just left. If he likes his meal he does a drawing on the tablecloth for Papa as

a tip, and you've only gone and thrown it on the fire. He's only the most famous painter in the world. Idiot! Imbecile!" She was in tears now. Everyone in the restaurant had stopped eating and gone quite silent.

Then Uncle Bruno was striding towards us, not his jolly self at all. "What is it?" he asked Amandine. "What's the matter?"

"It was Yannick, Papa," she cried. "He threw it on the fire, the tablecloth, the drawing."

"Had you told him about it, Amandine?" Uncle Bruno asked. "Did Yannick know about how sometimes he sketches something on the tablecloth, and how he leaves it behind for us?"

Amandine looked at me, her cheeks wet with tears. I thought she was going to lie. But she didn't.

"No, Papa," she said, lowering her head.

"Then you shouldn't be blaming him, should you, for something that was your fault. Say sorry to Yannick now." She mumbled it but she never raised her eyes. Uncle Bruno put his arm round me and walked me away. "Never mind, Yannick," he said. "He said he particularly liked his crème brûlée. That's probably why he left the drawing. You made the crème brûlée, didn't you? So it was for you really he did it. Always look on the bright side. For a moment you had in your hands a drawing done for you and your crème brûlée by the greatest painter in the world. That's something you'll never forget."

Later on as I came out of the bathroom I heard Amandine crying in her room. I hated to hear her crying, so I knocked on the door and went in. She was lying curled up on her bed hugging her pillow.

"I'm sorry," I said. "I didn't mean to upset you." She had stopped crying by now.

"It wasn't your fault, Yannick," she said, still sniffling a bit. "It's just that I hate it when Papa's cross with me. He hardly ever is, only when I've done something really bad. I shouldn't have blamed you. I'm sorry."

And then she smiled at me. Amandine smiled at me!

I lay awake all that night, my mind racing. Somehow I was going to put it all right again. I was going to make Amandine happy. By morning I had worked out exactly what I had to do and how to do it, even what I was going to say when the time came.

That morning, I didn't go for my walk in the hills. Instead I made my way down through the village towards the chateau. I'd often wondered what it was like behind those closed gates. Now I was going to find out. I waited till there was no one about, no cars coming. I climbed the gates easily enough, then ran down through the trees. And there it was, immense and forbidding, surrounded by forest on all sides. And there he was, the old man with very little hair I had seen the night before. He was sitting alone in the sunshine at the foot of the steps in front of the chateau, and he was sketching. I approached as

silently as I could across the grass, but somehow
I must have disturbed him. He looked up, shading
his eyes against the sun. "Hello, young man," he
said. Now that I was this close to him I could
see he was indeed old, very old, but his eyes were
young and bright and searching.

"Are you Monsieur Cézanne?" I asked him. "Are you the famous painter?" He seemed a little puzzled at this, so I went on. "My mother says you are the greatest painter in the world."

He was smiling now, then laughing. "I think

your mother's probably right," he said. "You clearly have a wise mother, but what I'd like to know is why she let a young lad like you come wandering here on his own?"

As I explained everything and told him why I'd come and what I wanted, he looked at me very intently, his brow furrowing. "I remember you now, from last night," he said, when I'd finished. "Of course I'll draw another picture for Bruno. What would he like? No. Better still, what would you like?"

"I like sailing boats," I told him. "Can you do boats?"

"I'll try," he replied with a smile.

It didn't take him long. He drew fast, never once looking up. But he did ask me questions as he worked, about where I'd seen sailing boats, about where I lived in Paris. He loved Paris, he said, and he loved sailing boats too.

"There," he said, tearing the sheet from his sketchbook and showing me. "What do you think?" Four sailing boats were racing over the sea out beyond a lighthouse, just as I'd seen them in Brittany. But I saw he'd signed it *Picasso*.

"I thought your name was Cézanne," I said.

He smiled up at me. "How I wish it was," he

49

said sadly. "How I wish it was. Off you go now."

I ran all the way back to the village, wishing all the time I'd told him that I was the one who had made the crème brûlée he'd liked so much. I found Amandine by the washing line, a clothes

peg in her mouth. "I did it!" I cried breathlessly, waving the drawing at her. "I did it! To make up for the one I burned."

Amandine took the peg out of her mouth and looked down at the drawing.

"That's really sweet of you to try, Yannick," she said. "But the thing is, it's got to be done by him, by Picasso himself. It's no good you drawing a picture and then just signing his name. It's got to be by him or it's not worth any money."

I was speechless. Then as she turned away to hang up one of Uncle Bruno's aprons, Aunt Mathilde came out into the garden with a basket of washing under her arm.

"Yannick's been very kind, Maman," said Amandine. "He's done me a drawing. After what happened last night. It's really good."

Aunt Mathilde had put down her washing

and was looking at the drawing. "Bruno!" she called. "Bruno, come out here!" And Uncle Bruno appeared, his hands white with flour. "Look at this," said Aunt Mathilde. "Look what Yannick did, and all by himself too."

Bruno peered at it closely for a moment, then started to roar with laughter. "I don't think so," he said. "Yannick may be a genius with crème brûlée, but this is by Picasso, the great man himself. I promise you. Isn't it, Yannick?"

So I told them the whole story. When I'd finished, Amandine came over and hugged me. She had tears in her eyes. I was in seventh heaven,

and Uncle Bruno waggled his moustache and gave me six crystallized apricots. Unfortunately Aunt Mathilde hugged me too and pinched my cheek especially hard. I was the talk of the inn that night, and felt very proud of myself. But best

of all Amandine came on my walk in the hills the next day and climbed trees with me and collected acorns, and held my hand all the way back down the village street, where everyone could see us, even the motor-scooter boys in their blue jeans.

·   ·   ·

They still have the boat drawing by Picasso hanging in the inn. Amandine runs the place now. It's as good as ever. She married someone else, as cousins usually do. So did I. I'm a writer still trying to follow in Jean Giono's footsteps. As for Cézanne, was my mother right? Is he the greatest painter in the world? Or is it Picasso? Who knows? Who cares? They're both wonderful and I've met both of them – if you see what I'm saying.

Tomas hates school, hates books and hates libraries.
But the stories spun by the Unicorn Lady draw
him in, making themselves part of him ... and
changing the course of his life for ever.

"This book needs to be bought for every library,
school and home, to share with as many children
as we can, that they might experience its magic
for themselves." *The Bookseller*

When cub reporter Lesley is sent to Venice
to interview a world-renowned violinist, she
discovers a long-kept secret – and learns how
one group of musicians survived the full horror
of war through music.

"Beautifully illustrated, this is a moving tale
of secrets, lies and the past." *The Independent*

When young Michael spots a whale on the
shores of the Thames, he is sure he must be
dreaming. But not only is the creature real
... it has a message for him.

"A thought-provoking, touching story
with beautiful illustrations on every page."
Primary Times

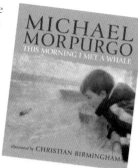

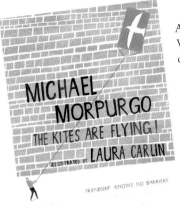

A television reporter's experiences in the West Bank reveal how children's hopes and dreams for peace can fly higher than any wall dividing communities and religions.

"Insightful and beautifully illustrated."
Daily Express

Michael loves to visit Mrs Pettigrew in her railway carriage by the sea, where she lives with her donkey, dogs and hens. But when plans are made to build a nuclear power station, Mrs Pettigrew's idyllic life becomes threatened – and Michael learns that nothing can ever stay the same.

"Amid the tears are sweet illustrations, a deep vein of humanity and very grown-up lessons about progress." *Observer*

Michael Morpurgo was 2003–2005 Children's Laureate, has written over one hundred books and is the winner of numerous awards, including the Whitbread Children's Book Award, the Blue Peter Book Award, the Smarties Book Prize and the Red House Children's Book Award. His books are translated and read around the world and his hugely popular novel *War Horse*, already a critically acclaimed stage play, is now also a blockbuster film. Michael and his wife, Clare, founded the charity Farms for City Children and live in Devon.

François Place completed his first illustrations for the Découverte Cadet series after studying visual expression at l'École Estienne, and his art has since illuminated numerous texts, including Michael Morpurgo's bestselling *War Horse* and Timothée de Fombelle's *Toby Alone* and *Toby and the Secrets of the Tree*. François is also an author in his own right, and among his credits are the highly praised *The Old Man Mad About Drawing*, *The Last Giants* and *The Atlas of the Geographers of Orbae*.